THE CURSED WELL

DHEERAJ KUMAR

ISBN 979-888521874-0

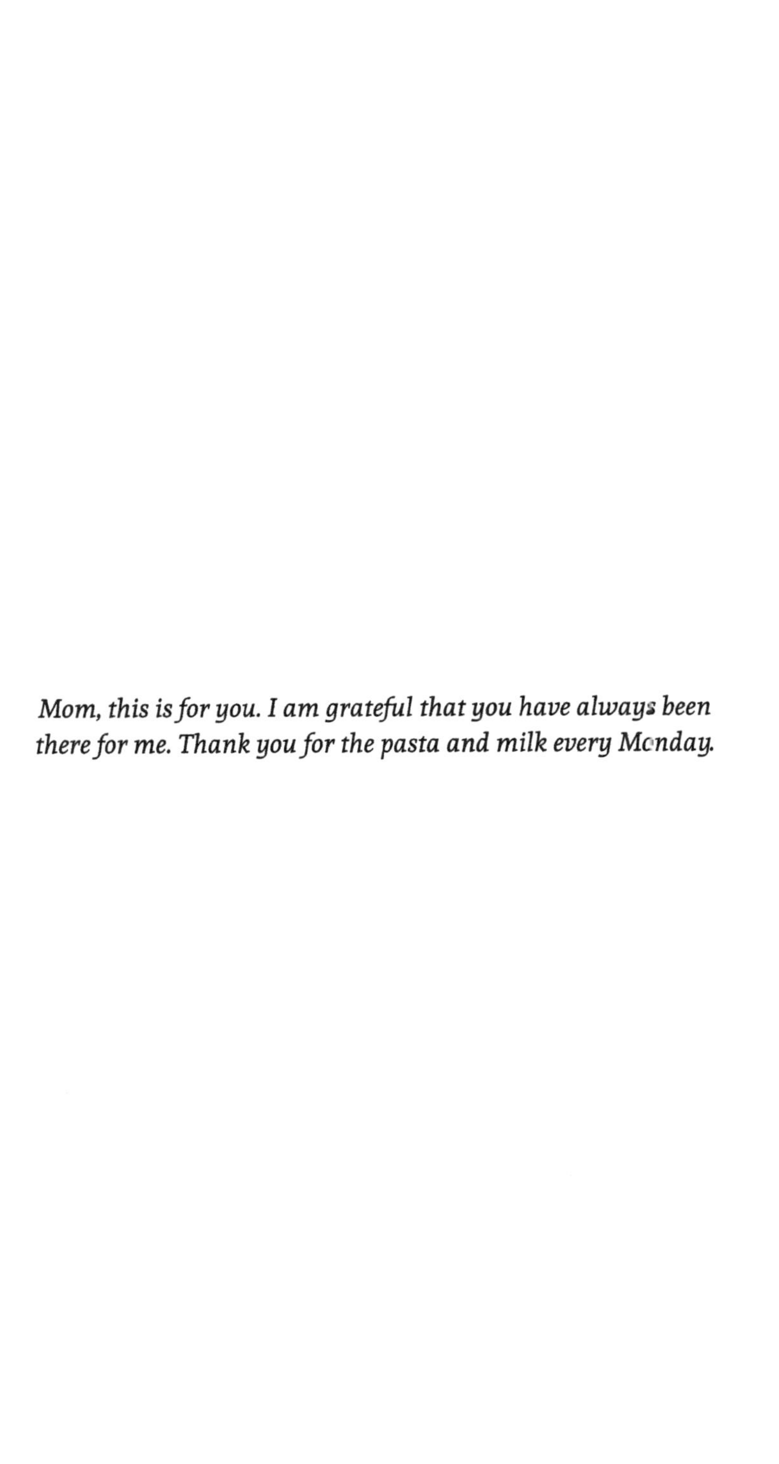

Mom, this is for you. I am grateful that you have always been there for me. Thank you for the pasta and milk every Monday.

Contents

1

Once upon a time in a village far up and in the mountains, something happened and this event very much changed life in this village, it changed it for the better. The tale of this village will be told in the story I am about to tell you. Please listen so you do not miss any significant points in this story.

There was once a village where people lived in harmony with their neighbors and didn't fight or cause any problems.

This village was also rich in gold. Gold was stuck there, and they built a mine to help them get more gold. It was because of this gold that this city became popular. Several villages came to see the gold mine and worked for the village as well.

Some other villages came to buy the gold from the people; this made the people of the village very rich. As rich as they were, none of them were greedy; they shared what they had and had no reason to doubt each other. They lived truthfully and shared their food with their fellow community members, no matter how small it might be; they didn't let any child feel neglected.

The Raja of the village was a very wise man who could control his people in case any dispute ever tried to come up. However, that rarely happened with his people because they took to his word and respected him, his wives, and his children. The Raja was the one who suggested they sell the gold to other villages and use the money gotten from gold sales to maintain their villages.

The money they made, they rarely spent it, and they just kept it in a safe at the Raja's house in case any member of the community needed it. If the miner at the Gold mine found any gold, they did not keep it for themselves, but rather they thought of their community first. This attitude made them love each other very deeply. Nothing could tear them apart, even if the other villages tried to offer some of the miner's money to try to steal the gold for them, but the miners all refused; the gold was too important to their people.

The people of that village saw the gold as a gift from the Earth Mother who had given it to her children to help them live better. They worshipped the Earth, and now she had rewarded them with a gift that would make them the envy of everyone. They bore sacrifices to the Earth Mother and didn't try to disrepute or desecrate her land.

The land in that village was very scared, and no one was allowed to speak badly on the soil or even spill any human blood on that land in the fear that the Earth Mother would be angry at them and cause the Earth to cave in and swallow their village whole. But as peaceful and loveable as this village can be, there were people that wanted to take over and run them out of their homes.

There was another village on the other side of the river. Their land was very dry, and they had to buy everything they ate from the other villages. This village had hated in its heart for the village that had gold. They hated that the Earth Mother had bestowed upon them the gold that should have been theirs, but instead, she gave them dry land where nothing grew on it.

The Raja of this village wanted to see what the fuss was all about, so he arranged a courtesy visit to the village where the gold was. He wanted to tour their mines and take in the capacity of the village. The other village welcomed him with open hands, and they took him in their homes, both him and his entourage.

When the Raja arrived at the villages, he was shocked at how fresh everything was, the very atmosphere was very cool, and everything was just perfect. They took him to the chef's house, and they all had a feast with the villagers. The Raja's wives were very hospitable and made their food and gave them a place to sleep for the night. They promised to take them on a tour of their Gold mine the next day.

The next day the Raja was very eager to see the gold mine and its contents; he was so excited that even the villagers could see it. The two chefs and their guards went all the way to the mind, and the mine was far more appealing than the village itself. It was a long stretch of land underground; most of it had been dug by the miners but getting into the main room of the mine, the chef opened his mouth as he looked at the beauty of the mine.

The gold was everywhere, stuck in the wall and the ground; it glowed in the dark, and it was very beautiful. The Raja couldn't have been more filled with jealousy; the gold was supposed to be their gold, their land. He just kept smiling at the Raja and remarked that the mine was, in fact, very impressive, and he was happy that the Earth Mother had given them that gift.

In the other village, Raja picked up a very big gold piece and gave it to Raja as a symbol of respect and a gift to his people. The Raja saw it as an insult, but he smiled politely and accepted the gold piece.

He was so angry that he didn't wait anymore in the village; the Raja said he had to leave that day because he had matters to take care of back in his village. The villagers saw him off and packed other gifts to take with him when he returned to these people. Before dusk that day, the Raja returned to his village, and the villagers gathered to welcome him.

But when he arrived, he didn't greet anyone; he just went straight into his house and immediately called a meeting of his subjects. He also ordered that any gifts the other village gave him be burnt. The Raja subjects were immediately gathered in a room in the Raja's house, and he was not happy at all.

"How dare he?" The Raja shouted as he walked up and down the room.

"You have to calm down," Roshan, the Raja's right-hand man, said, "what happened where you went?"

“You want to know what happened." The Raja shouted, "okay I will tell you what happened. First of all, why is it so damn hot?" the Raja said, fanning himself with his hand as he took a seat.

"The sun’s ray is hitting us directly now, it is that time of the year," Pawan, the Raja’s adviser on the climate, said.

"You see what I am talking about. Do you know I didn’t for one moment sweat when I was at the other village visiting them? I didn’t even common about the sun; it was so cool and calm. Why can’t we have that here?" the Raja complained.

"Well, we live in two different parts of the land. They live down to the river and we lived a little far away from it," Pawan said again.

"Oh, shit up Pawan!" The Raja exclaimed, "their land is so pure and full of life and ours is desolate because of our stupid forefathers who offended the Earth Mother but it will soon change don’t worry about that?" The Raja said.

"So did you see it?" Amar, the Raja advisor on village life, asked him.

"Oh yes I did," the Raja said with his eyes gleaming.

"Was it as magnificent as they said it was?" Roshan asked, leaning closer to the Raja. He was the one seated closest to the Raja because he was the right-hand man.

"Yes, and it was glorious," the Raja replied, recalling the gold mine he saw. "There was Gold everywhere, on the floor, the walls, and even the roof. The Raja even gave me this gold piece" the Raja brought out the gold piece from a pouch he had in his hand.

His subjects, four men, gasped at the gold piece; it was marvelous, Pawan wanted to reach for it, but the Raja told him not to.

"That is poison right there," the Raja said.

"How?" Roshan asked.

"He gave me that gold piece to say they are richer than us and we can only afford the scraps from their land. But that is about to change," the Raja said, looking at the last man in the room. His name was Ramesh, and he was the most notorious man in the village.

"How is it going to change?" Ramesh asked. "Because my dear Ramesh, you are willing to help me take that village?" The Raja said, smiling.

"It will be an honor my Raja" Ramesh smiled back at the Raja.

Over the weeks, the Raja informed Ramesh of the lay of the land of the other village during his tour of the village. He made sure to note down the way the land was shaped. Ramesh took in this information and came up with a plan to take the village.

Ramesh presented it back to the Raja, and he held a meeting with his most loyal subjects; they had the meeting in the dead of night, locked the door, and made sure no one was listening in on their conversation. They didn't know who to trust presently, and the other village might have spies watching them.

“Ramesh, tell them what you have," the Raja said.

"Okay, my Raja," Ramesh said, placing a piece of cloth on the slab of stone in the middle of the room; the slab of stone served as the table; it was elected and stood at four feet. Ramesh unrolled the cloth and on it was a drawing that looked like a map.

"This is the plan that we will use to take the city. I have formulated a two-way plan rather simple they will not see us coming. We will take them from the entrance and also from the Gold mine became it is the closest to the outskirt of the village. Seize the gold mine and you have the village,"

Ramesh explained his plan.

The Raja asked, "And what about an escape plan?".

"You were the one who said you wanted to take the city" Ramesh smiled at the Raja. "It's either we take the city, or we die trying. There is no way out," Ramesh said.

"Ramesh, you cold man," the Raja said and laughed.

The meeting was concluded, and the subjects dispersed to their homes. Two weeks later, they went on the road to storm the village. Five thousand men marched from their village, crossed the river, and arrived at the Gold village.

The scouts of the Gold Village saw them approaching and quickly went to inform the Raja, who formed a party together to meet the man and asked them what their terms what.

When the Raja saw the other Raja, he was surprised and asked why he wanted to storm their city.

"To take over it, of course, we have spent too much time living in a land that has nothing to offer us. We want to enjoy the gold too," the Raja said and smiled.

Suddenly they heard cries in the village; Ramesh and his men were attacking the Gold mine.

"What have you done? The Raja looked at him in horror.

"What I should have done a long time ago," the Raja said.

"May the Earth Mother curse you."

"She has done so for a long time," another Raja said and uttered a battle cry.

His men began to storm the village while the Raja had to watch in horror as his village was invaded, houses were burned, and people were slaughtered on the very ground they stood. The men entered houses and slaughtered anyone they saw in their sight; the Gold village didn't stand a chance.

Ramesh's men took over the Gold mine and forced the men and made them kneel at the entrance of the Gold Mine. The Raja left the fighting and made his way to the Gold mine, where he met the men kneeling outside. He offered them a choice.

"You can either join me or you can die. Pick one."

The men looked at each other, and in their hearts, they made the choice that they all had to. The men looked at the Raja and didn't utter a word.

"You are still loyal to a village that is about to fall under my command?" the Raja asked the men.

The men still said nothing; they would never betray their homeland.

"Okay then, Ramesh, do whatever you want with these men," the Raja said and turned to leave.

As he departed from the gold mine, he heard the man's screams as Ramesh slaughtered them all. He went to the center of the villagers, where the survivors were rounded up, including the former Raja.

The Raja got up on the podium in the middle of the village, and he addressed the people.

"People of Gold village, hear me for I have come to take over from you. You have lived on this land for years while my people had to wallow in nothing and suffer on barren land, victims of the foolish actions of our ancestors. Well now we are tired, and we have come to live here, in this land that is cool and peaceful," the Raja announced.

"You will never find peace or even a home here," the former Raja spat on the floor. He was kneeling on the ground like the other survivors, and his hand was bound to the back.

"I will build a new home for my people here," the Raja said as he left the podium and walked over to the Raja.

"Why are you doing this? We can all co-exist in peace," the former Raja cried.

"In peace? You mean you will turn our people into slaves, and we will watch you prosper and leave us behind. No that can never happen, it's either we are in control or nothing." The Raja shouted.

"I hope you find whatever form of peace you are looking for and let me tell you when you do, you will be disappointed."

"I have found it and it came in form of your land and it's your mine. It is rather beautiful," the Raja said.

"Kill them all," the Raja said and walked away from the former Raja.

"The Earth Mother will avenge us," the former Raja screamed out as one of the soldiers moved towards him.

The survivor's screams were heard as their throats were slashed. Ramesh walked into the village just as the survivors were killed.

"Is that all?" the Raja asked Ramesh.

"Yes, the entire Gold village has been killed," Ramesh said smiling.

"Then it is done, the Gold village is ours," the Raja said and smiled. He held a hand up, and his men cheered; they had a new home.

Unknowing to the Raja, a group of people survived from the village. While the Raja went off to the Gold mine and before the Raja was captured, he secretly rounded up a group of people that he could find, and he told them to run for the mountains and never look back and forget they had a home here. He gave them some money and told them he was very sorry he couldn't protect them anymore.

This group of people ran through the mountains, cowering in the dark as they heard the distant screams of their people being killed. None of them dared to leave the cave; they spent the night in the cave. By day, the man who was put in charge of the survivors, Veer, said it was safe for them to leave; the people asked him, and he said he didn't know, but they had to keep moving.

The people followed Veer as he led them from their former home; as they left, they took one last look at where their home was and all they saw was black smoke rising. They all felt sadness in their hearts, but they had to keep moving.

Veer led them farther and farther away from the mountains, and one day they came upon a clearing; although it was dry land and no one lived there, Veer told them to make camp there, and he said Mother Earth had guided them there. But there was one problem in this land; they found no stream or river to provide them with water. They needed water to survive, and if this land didn't give them water, they would have to move on.

Veer to them not to worry that the Earth Mother brought them that far and wouldn't give up on them. He told them to pray and go to sleep that she would help them; the next morning, Veer suddenly woke at the crack of dawn: he had heard someone calling his name softly.

He stood from where he slept and followed the voice; the voice led him to a well. As he stood above the well and looked in, it was like the water was trying to tell him something.

"This water will serve your people and give them life again. Make this your new home and call it Thar. It will be a home for people that have been kicked out of their homes. Guard it well," the voice said.

"Yes, Earth Mother" Veer closed his eyes and smiled; the Earth Mother would never forsake her children.

The rest of the survivors woke, and Veer led them to the well. They all rejoiced and drank the water from the well and watched their faces; they all thanked the Earth Mother for their present and went on to set up their new home.

As the Earth Mother said, their new home would be a Thar for people who were displaced, and they received a lot of people and helped them with a home.

2

The people of the Thar built a home that could accommodate people from far and wide, people heard about their village and how it is hospitable, and the people are very good; natives trooped there by the hundreds, people that have been run out of their homes by the Raja of their other village as he went about expanding his empire to the other village. He burnt down villages and killed people, took their wives and women as wives for his soldiers, and took their children as slaves. It was a very bad time, and the people trooped to Thar, the one place the Raja couldn't get them no matter how much he tried because the Earth Mother had protected the land.

With the new people that came in also came new cultures and traditions, people with different gods and beliefs coming together to stay in harmony, the village of Thar had only one rule that they all respected the Earth Mother even if they did not worship her, they asked the people to respect their beliefs and not speak badly of the Earth Mother.

The people complied, and the village was very peaceful. The villagers got to see innovation from other people and learned about their way of life. They exchanged knowledge on medicine, farming, food, and livestock; the village then had a commercial atmosphere. People started to have farms; some started to breed livestock to sell them; a commercial marketplace was built for the traders and with it came development. The news of the village spread far and wide, and education eventually came into the village.

The children of the village had to learn informally; they would converge under a huge tree at the center of the village where several instructors would teach them about the history and also about Geography, knowing the lay of the land, how to know if rain was coming, how to know a land that will bear fruit from one that is barren. The children listened attentively and took in all the information.

A leadership system was put in place after Veer declined the role of the Raja saying he wasn't meant to lead the people to their new home, 12 elders were chosen from the village to form a committee to help the villagers make decisions and guide them, Veer agreed to be part of that committee, and he served well.

He eventually married one of the women from one of the tribes that came to settle down in Thar. The woman caught his fancy one day as he sat in front of his house. She was coming back from the Well and had a clay pot on her head he saw her and took a liking to her immediately. He asked around to see who she was. He found out she had a father, and he was a man who hated men looking at his daughter.

Getting the man to let Veer marry his daughter was tricky; Veer approached the man himself and the hot thrown out of the man's house, But Veer didn't give up, he likes the mind daughter, so he watched her whenever she went to the stream. Her voice was angelic, and her laughter was soothing.

Veer found himself daydreaming about this fine beauty, he approached the remaining people in the ruling committee, and they all went to the man's house to ask for his daughter in marriage. On getting to the man's house, he was shocked to see the ruling elders and asked what they wanted; they told him they were there to talk about his daughter's hand in marriage. The man looked around and saw Veer in their midst.

"I have told you to say away from my home," the man shouted as he saw Veer. He took off his slippers and wanted to throw them at Veer when one of the elders held his hand and told him to take a seat.

The remaining elders took a seat too, and they were served water by the man's wife and his daughter. Veer got a glimpse of his beloved, she smiled a shy smile at him, and Veer smiled back at her. Her father saw this and told her to get back inside the house.

"You see, this man has come to us and he told us he is interested in marrying your daughter," one of the elders started to say.

"I thank you for all your coming, but I cannot release my daughter to be married to any man," the man responded.

"You can't keep her in your home forever, you will have to let her go someday and who better than the man who led the very first set of natives to this land. A man that has been blessed by the Earth Mother herself," a second elder said.

"He is a very respectable man, but I still cannot release my daughter for marriage," the man said stubbornly.

"Why won't you let her marry me?" Veer asked the man speaking up. "I promise not to let anything bad happen to her," Veer said, looking at the man in his eyes.

"The heart of men is evil, and I do not want my sweet daughter to be a victim," the man answered him.

"If the heart of men is evil, that means your heart must be evil too," Veer said, and the man gasped, looking at him with wide eyes.

"Look, if you are not evil then surely you will know that not all men are like that. I am of pure intentions," Veer said.

The man thought it over in his head and called his daughter; she emerged from the house with a shy smile on her face.

"So, what do you think of this man?" The man asked, pointing at Veer.

"Father, he is a very kind man and I think he is rather a good-looking gentleman," she answered.

"I am glad you think so because that is your husband to be," the man said.

"Really?" she exclaimed, "Thank you so much father" she hugged her father.

Veer smiled, and so did the elders who followed him; he finally got what he wanted. The two of them got married two weeks later. The whole village was in attendance, and many people gave their blessings to the ceremony, including the Earth Mother, for it rained on the morning of the wedding. Veer and his wife went on to be respected members of this village, and they had lots of children.

The story of Veer and his wife was told from generation to generation in this village as the village of Thar expanded into a small town. The small town of Thar revered Veer for how he led the people to a new home. Veer was dead for a long time already, but his name still lived on amongst the people; his story was taught in schools as part of history.

The town has much developed now; there were proper schools even if they were still substandard. The businesses in the village had also expanded, with the traders having their shops on the street corners.

They no longer had the 12 elders ruling system, they came together to elect a Raja to oversee the village's affairs, and although they voted, the Rajataincy has always been from the bloodline of Veer.

Now it was his great-grandson that was the Raja of the village. His name was Amir, and he was loved although when he became the Raja but no doubt as every inch wise as the people who came before him. The people of Thar didn't worship the Earth Mother as they did before, but they still acknowledged her and respected her in the village.

There was a shrine in the middle of the village for her, near a waterfall erected there in memory of Veer; the village would often go to the shrine and ask for favors from the Earth Mother. They still used the Well as one of their major sources of water and also the rain that the Earth Mother blessed them with from time to time.

Whenever it rains, because of how dry the land is, the residents would put out buckets to collect the rainwater to use for cooking and washing.

The Well was seen as a symbol in the village, and nobody ever deserted the area, they weren't allowed to wait for shoes when they went near the Well, and children and menstruating women weren't allowed near the water at all.

But then again, something happened at the Well long after Veer had died. The Earth Mother appeared to the Raja in a trance and informed him of a certain evil on the land that wanted to take their water.

The Raja asked the Earth Mother what they should do to protect their water; the Earth told him not to be frightened that she would take care of her people. She told the Raja to go back to his people and informed them to stay in their homes on the seventeenth day of that month.

The Raja woke and immediately told one of his guards to go around the village sharing this information. He instructed the guard to tell the villagers to fetch water down and make sure they finished all their business before the seventeenth day as they were not going to be allowed out of their homes on the seventeenth.

The villagers all scampered to fetch their water; there was a long queue at the Well as people rushed. Traders made sure they finished all the traders, and farmers made sure they sold all their wares before going inside their homes and locking the doors behind them.

On the seventeenth, the whole village woke up in anticipation of what was going to happen. They all looked outside from their windows to try to see what was going to happen. They kept looking and looking, but nothing happened. The Raja himself was getting confused about what the Earth Mother told him.

But as soon as it was noon, something happened that shocked the people, they saw a woman walk into the village, she looked weary and tired, and her clothes were filled with dust as she had just trekked down from the mountain. One of the Raja's wives wants to go out and help this woman, but the Raja tells her to stay put in the house.

The whole village watched the woman walk in the direction of the Well; they all saw her fetch a pail of water from the Well and sip from it; she also used it to wash her face and her feet when she was doing that, she turned. Everyone gasped in their homes; she looked very beautiful. The dust on her face had concealed her features, but now they were visible. The woman took one last look at the water and started to walk away. She walked out of the village and back into the mountains where she emerged from.

The villagers still stayed inside the house till night that day, they were in disbelief about what had happened. The Raja went to sleep that day, and the Earth Mother came to him again. She told him the woman had come to conquer the evil in the water, and they should all celebrate tomorrow with a feast. The Earth Mother also told the priest that from now, the villagers weren't allowed out on the seventeenth day of the month and that if anyone tries to fetch water from the Well that day, that person will go blind and eventually die if they do so.

The Raja said he understood all she had said and thanked her for her projection. The whole village woke to the sound of the Raja's guards going around the village, telling them they were all invited to a feast at the Raja's house.

They all bathed and put on their nice clothes and headed to the Raja's house where his wives were cooking food in large pots and his sons were skinning meat and roasting them on a spit; the Raja called the villagers together before they started to feast and addressed them on what the goddess had said to him.

"People of Thar, the Earth Mother has asked me to congratulate you," the Raja said, "She tells me the evil that has plagued our well is over."

The whole village cheered hearing this from the Raja.

"As I was saying the Earth Mother asked us to hold this feast in honor of her. She helped in vanquishing this evil and in doing so, she has a few rules she would like us to adhere to," the Raja said.

"What does the Earth Mother want?" Someone shouted from the crowd, "we will do whatever she wants" the village agreed with this person that spoke.

"Okay put Earth Mother wants us to stay in our homes on the seventeenth of every month. She says the evil in the Well will be back."

The village gasped.

"Don't worry, she is still with us. The woman who came yesterday which I'm sure we all saw will come back to help us vanquish the evil in our well," the Raja explained to the people.

"And what happened if we do not do this?"

"The Earth Mother is going to get angry, and she won't help us anymore," the Raja said.

"And if anyone gets close to the Well and looks at it on the seventeenth day of the month, the Earth Mother will make the person go blind and that person will eventually die. So please help me in making sure that the Earth Mother is happy with us, and she isn't angry at what we choose to do in this village," the Raja begged the villagers.

They looked at him, and they all agreed to adhere to this rule because they didn't want to lose their eyesight or even die. So, it became a tradition; on the seventeenth day of each month, the villages all locked their homes and waited for the lady to help conquer the evil that lay in the Well.

The villagers also reported that when they went to the Well early in the morning on the eighteenth day, the water in the Well would look bloody like someone had been murdered inside it. They wouldn't be able to use the water until they had feasted at the Raja's house. They had this feast on the eighteenth day of every month, and it was until they were done that they could now go to the Well and use the clear water. This continued over the years, and the villagers passed on this tradition to their children, and their children passed it down to their children until now.

Although they have several legends as to whom the lady in the mountain was, she was still as young as she came into the village for the first time; she didn't age or even look old.

Just the same way she walked in and the same clothes every time, stories began to circulate on who she was; some stories said she was the spirit of the Erath Mother who had come to help them.

Some say she was a mystical spirit the Erath Mother had sent down to help the people, and she couldn't age because she wasn't human. Others said she was from a tribe of people who lived deep in the mountain, a tribe that civilization hasn't met yet, a tribe that has been in hiding and held the very secret to life itself. Other stories circulated also, but the one that took root the most in the people was a very peculiar story.

The sure goes as; thus, the woman came from a tribe who lived on this land before, but something happened that forced them to live in the mountains, the woman's husband was killed and his body was dumped into the Well, and this polluted the Well which made the people leave their home to live in the mountains.

Now the woman comes down on the seventeenth day of the month to meet her husband at the Well; they say he calls for her, and she hears his cries and descends from her place amongst her people to be with him for that one day. They also said she cried to the Earth Mother in anguish after losing her husband at the Well.

The Earth Mother heard her prayer and helped her by bringing her husband's soul to the Well every seventeenth day of the month; he could descend from the heavens to be with her. The woman would then wash her face with the water and her feet, she would feel relaxed after then, and she would return to be back the next month.

The people sympathized with this woman, the anguish of coming here once a month to be with who she loved. They also said the reason the Well was always blood like the next morning was back up, the husband was returning to the heavens, and the Earth Mother was reminding the people of the atrocity committed on that land.

The now modern town of this village still waits for the woman in the mountain to descend; some people have said they could hear soft crying whenever she came. They said she was mourning her late husband.

Once a group of men from the town wanted to go into the mountains and find the mystery woman's tribe, but they left and never came back to the town. The town people just assumed they died of starvation in the mountains, but the truth was the men did find the tribe in the mountains, but they weren't allowed to go back to their people because they would betray the location of the tribe; a tribe that has lived in the mountains for almost 500 years.

Life in the village was good, and as a result of this, children were free to express themselves, they weren't forced to not speak in public anymore, and now that the people now knew about education in the town, children could go to school and learn all about the world.

They soon learned how to express themselves while talking in public, and they knew how to express their opinions and make sure they were heard whenever they were put in public.

Amongst these children were two teenagers, a boy, and a girl. The two of them were in the same class, and their families loved living side by side on a street. Since childhood, the two of them have been friends; they do everything together, eating, watching cartoons, reading, and even sleeping. Their families encouraged their friendship, and they grew up to be as thick as thieves.

They were both intelligent in their way, and they got the best grades in their class. But one thing was paramount to the two of them; they both made a pact not to be with anyone until they were both done with school because they wanted to focus on their education and nothing but that alone.

The boy was called Neel, and the girl was called Muskan. They were the apple of their parent's eyes. But as far as friendships go, there will come a time where they will be tested. Muskan had developed a tiny crush on Neel, but she didn't know how to tell him because of the past the two of them had.

She started to dress more provocatively to get his attention, and she went to his house even at odd hours to get his attention, but Neel wasn't interested in that type of relationship. All he wanted was to be the best student in school and get awards.

Muskan started to lag in her studies because she was trying so hard to please Neel. She wanted only him to be the top student, so she started failing on purpose, which Neel didn't like; he asked her why she was falling, and she said she was having struggles, so Neel agreed to tutor her, which she loved because it made him spend more time with her.

But it all changed one day when they got a new addition to their class, a new girl. Her family had just moved into town, and she had to start school.

The teacher brought her on a bright and sunny day and introduced her to the class as Prita. The boys whopped as Prita was introduced to the class, she was a pretty girl with full bosoms, and her skin practically shone. The boys went out of their way to be nice to get, and one of them was Neel. He offered her a seat beside him, much to the disgust of Muskan, who sat in front of him.

Muskan disliked Neel being nice to Prita because she felt Prita was prettier than her and might want to take his attention away from her. Prita did exactly that, although she didn't do it on purpose; she so smote Neel that he didn't think of Muskan anymore. He would stay with her in school after everyone had gone home, claiming he just wanted to help her study more. Muskan would go back home alone after school, something she hadn't done before. She and Neel always came back home from school together.

The school noticed this and started to secretly call Neel and Prita a couple, which Muskan hated, and she confronted Neel with his information.

"Wow, they are calling us that?" Neel had laughed in her face when Muskan asked him, "you know that is not true, we are just friends. I am only helping her get more accustomed to our town," Neel explained to her.

"Let one of the other boys do it then, why does it have to be you?" Muskan shouted at him.

"Oh my, are you jealous of me spending time with her instead of you?" Neel joked, "Muskan," Neel said as he put a hand on his shoulder. "You are my best friend and that won't change. This thing with Prita and I is just temporary, there is nothing to be jealous of."

"Okay, I guess," Muskan said.

They were alone in the classroom, and it was after school; Prita had appeared at the door, and Muskan saw her and scowled.

"Okay, Muskan, I have to go now, be good okay," Neel said and carried his backpack, leaving her standing while he went to meet Prita.

"You are leaving with her," Muskan called him back. "I thought we were supposed to walk back together," Muskan shouted.

"Sorry but the plan has changed, I am asking Prita to the market instead, she wants to see the sights, don't worry we will walk to school together tomorrow," Neel said and left with Prita who just waved at Muskan.

Muskan was so angry that she walked straight home, went into her room, and carried herself to sleep. The next day at school, she went over to Neel's house so they could walk to school together, but his mom told her Neel had left with someone already.

Muskan knew it was Prita immediately, and she was so furious, she stormed to school and reached there earlier than she was supposed to. She wanted to go into their class and cry her eyes out before everyone else came, but she saw Prita and Neel kissing on one of the tables when she walked in.

Muskan was shocked at this, but she didn't confront them; she just withdrew silently from the classroom and ran to the bathroom to cry, so much for pacts between best friends.

"I will make sure that bitch pays for what she did to me," Muskan said in between sobs.

For the rest of the day, Muskan avoided Neel and Prita; she didn't sit with them in the class and made sure she sat far away from them at lunch.

Neel asked what was wrong with her, and she lied that she was on her period, so she had mood swings. Prita came over and told her sorry, but Muskan just turned up her head until Prita left.

ᑭᑭᑭ

After school, Muskan met Neel and Prita and said she wanted to walk with them after school; Prita was delighted to bring her along. So, the three of them walked around the town after school, showing Prita their favorite places and telling her about their people's well.

Prita giggled as Neel made jokes, and Muskan winced as they laughed. She felt Prita was throwing herself all over Neel. They both followed Prita to her house, and she invited them inside her house. Neel and Muskan were received by her mother, who was happy that Prita was making friends in the town.

She invited them into their living room and served them tea. She asked how they were and how the school was; they spoke about Prita's town and their school there for some minutes.

Prita's mom told them to stay over for dinner, but Muskan declined, saying her mother needed her at home for some chores. Neel wanted to stay, but Muskan stepped on his foot, and he said he would follow Muskan home instead.

On their way home, Neel and Muskan spoke about Prita's home.

"She seems a nice person," Muskan said as they walked home.

"Yes, she is very nice, and I see where Prita got her manners from," Neel said.

"About Prita, is she like the official third member of our group now, or am I about to be thrown out of my best friend position?" Muskan asked Neel.

"Oh, come on, you are still in your position. Prita is a friend but I am hoping she becomes more than a friend," Neel said to Muskan.

"So, what do you mean?"

"I mean I want to ask her to be my girlfriend," Neel said.

"What are you serious, what about our pact?" Muskan shouted.

"Oh, that silly thing," Neel said.

"Oh, now it's a silly thing?" Muskan said.

"I'm sorry I said that but forget about that for now tell me how I can win her over."

"Don't ask me that I do not know how guys win girls over, I haven't had a boyfriend so I can't help you with that," Muskan said.

"Oh, I will ask the boys at school then," Neel said, and they continued walking.

They rounded the corner of their street, and Muskan told Neel she wouldn't be walking with him to school the next day.

"Why? What is going on?" Neel asked her.

"Nothing really, I just have some things to do and I might be late to school."

"Wow, that must be pretty important because you are not usually late to school. But I guess that's cool too, I will just walk with Prita to school."

"Okay cool," Muskan said.

Neel's house was just before Muskan's house, so she bade him goodbye and continued to her house.

The next morning while Neel was on his way to school, Muskan was looking at him from her room window, she had other things to do, but it didn't involve her staying at home. When Muskan saw him leave his house, she left her own house and stood safely from him as he walked to school; whenever he turned around, she would duck and hide somewhere until he continued walking.

She followed him to Prita's house, she saw him greet her, and they both walked to school. Muskan hid in a corner, and she was sure the two of them were long gone. She made her move; she walked confidently to Prita's house and knocked on the door.

"Hello, Muskan isn't it," Prita's mother said as she opened the door.

"Yes," Muskan smiled at her.

"I'm sorry but you just missed Prita and Neel. But I'm sure if you hurry, you might meet them."

"Oh, don't worry about that, I am not here about that, I am here to see about another matter," Muskan said.

"Oh, I hope there is no problem?"

"Oh no there isn't, can I come in please?" Muskan smiled sweetly.

"Yes sure, come on in" Prita's mother opened the door wide for Muskan to come in.

She saw her in the living room, and Muskan took a seat; Prita's mother went to fetch Muskan some tea while she waited.

Prita's father was on his way to work, and he saw Muskan seated in the living room.

"Who are you?" He asked her.

"That is one of Prita's new friends. Her name is Muskan," Prita's mother said as she brought tea for Muskan.

"Good morning, sir, how do you do?" Muskan greeted him politely.

"How do you do too?" Prita's father said, "May I ask why you are here?"

"I was about to ask her that too," Prita's mother said and sat in front of Muskan.

"Okay, you ask her that, I am leaving," Prita's father said, walking to the door.

"Before you leave sir, you might want to hear what I am about to say," Muskan called him back.

"Okay, what is it?" Prita's father said, turning around.

"Neel has been spending a lot of time with Prita as off late and I thought he was just helping her to know the town but I'm afraid it is more than that. Yesterday at school, I saw both of kissing in a classroom," Muskan said.

"That bastard," Prita's father swore.

"Are you sure this is true?" Prita's mother asked her.

"Yes, ma'am it is true and Prita had been to his house once," Muskan said.

"I will kill him, and his parent's" Prita's father shouted.

"I know his house address if you would like that," Muskan smiled, lifting the cup of tea to her lips.

She left Prita's house five minutes later; there was a huge grin on her face.

She was in a good mood that day, and Neel asked how she was.

"I am very good" Muskan smiled at him, she even played with Prita in school, and by the end of the day, they both had inside jokes.

Neel was happy the two of them were getting along, they sat together for lunch, and Prita had told Muskan that Neel had asked her to be his girlfriend when they both went to the Cafe.

"Oh, that is so amazing. I am so happy for you" Muskan hugged Prita and smiled the fakest smile ever.

"I know, thank you. He is really cute and so sweet but something is holding me back," Prita said.

"Oh, what is that?"

"I want to ask your permission before I start to date him. I know you were his best friend and you guys spent time together with each other, but I want to make sure I'm not intruding on anything," Prita said.

"Oh, Prita you are not intruding on anything. So, if I say you are intruding you won't date Neel?"

"Yes, I won't date Neel."

"Oh, Prita, Neel is happy with you, I don't want anything to stop him from being happy," Muskan said to Prita.

"Oh, thank you so much," Prita squealed. "I will inform him of my decision after school."

After school, Muskan left Neel and Prita alone, so she went home earlier and waited for the show that was about to happen.

Around evening that day, she heard a commotion happening in the steers, and she smiled, it had started, she looked out her window and saw Prita's father in front of Neel's house shouting at his father.

Muskan ran out of the house and saw her parents in front of Neel's house also. They were trying to calm Prita's father down.

"Stay away from my daughter," Prita's father shouted. "That is all I came to tell you" He spat on the ground and walked away.

Neel stood there in shock, and he couldn't even look at his parents, so he ran and took off. His parents and Muskan's parents tried to call him back, and Muskan told them she would go after him. Neel ran to a hill overlooking the town; he sat down on the ground and looked at the town.

"What was that all about?" Muskan asked Neel as she sat beside him. This was their special place; they came there together from time to time.

"Prita's father came to my house and told me to stay away from Prita but he doesn't know about us. Me and Prita just been a couple this afternoon."

"Wow, that is news to me" Muskan feigned ignorance.

"I mean who would have told him what was going on between me and Prita. Did you tell them anything?" Neel asked Muskan.

"Me? Come on, Neel, I would never do that. You know I want you to be happy Muskan lied, "I am offended you even thought that about me."

"I am sorry I asked you that, but this is very confusing. What can I do, he has banned Prita from walking to school with me or even seeing me," Neel said, holding his head in his hand?

"I might have an idea of what you can do," Muskan said.

"Oh," Neel looked up at her.

"Why don't you sneak to Prita's house while her parents are out and tell her to meet you outside on the day after tomorrow so you two can spend time together."

"Muskan that day is on the 17th, and you know we can't be out on the 17th."

"Oh, come on Neel, we can't be put in the town on the 17th but you can bring her here to this speculation place which technically isn't part of the town. You too can spend the day together and Prita can pretend that she is angry at her parents and lock the door of her room till night. When it is dark, the two of you can sneak out of the town then," Muskan said.

"I don't know Muskan this plan seems dangerous."

"Do you like Prita?" Muskan asked Neel.

"Come on, you know I do," Neel answered.

"Then you will fight for her and you will do this. The Earth Mother might even take pity on you since you are both lovers," Muskan said.

"That's true. Thank you Muskan I will do that," Jump said.

Of course, you would, Muskan smiled at him, and they sat there till it was dark and it was time to go home.

On the 17th, while everyone else was in their homes, Prita sneaked out to meet Neel at the secret spot on the hill. Neel had prepared a picnic for the two of them.

While the woman from the mountain came down to cleanse the well, Muskan smiled, knowing her plan was working very well. The woman left the village, and the next day while the whole town feasted, Prita and Neel's family couldn't find their children; they searched for them, but they didn't see them.

They were asked Muskan where they were, but she said she didn't know where they were. The town people organized a search party to find them, and they all went in different directions. In the evening of that day, there was a massive crowd in the town center, people were crying, and Prita's mother was screaming.

Neel and Prita came back to the town, but their corpses were brought into the town.

Muskan got there and smiled internally, she knew the Earth Mother punished them for disobeying the rule she laid down, and Muskan was happy because this was what she wanted; if she couldn't have Neel, then no one could have him too.

Prita's parents were devastated by the loss of their daughter that they packed up their belongings and left the town for good. Neel's parents were awash with grief, but Muskan consoled them playing the role too well.

After the Neel and Prita incident, people began to monitor their children closely, especially in the 17th; they would make sure they were home with them and weren't someplace else doing another thing.

Muskan didn't tell anyone she was the home that advised Neel to go outside with Prita that faithful day. She just kept quiet and enjoyed the sympathy that people showered her with. People pitied her everywhere she went, in the market and at school.

Her childhood friend had just died, and she played the role well; she stayed to herself in school and didn't talk to anyone. Even at home, she would lock herself in her room, refusing to eat or even drink any form of food; her parents begged her not to harm herself and pull her together for the sake of Neel.

Muskan listened to them and finally returned to normal, although she didn't want to show she was happy that Neel was dead. She was still mourning and acting like she was much damaged but inside, she was doing dances.

She didn't want them to die initially, but then they brought it upon themselves, and Neel was foolish to think the Earth Mother wouldn't punish them after she had told their ancestors not to leave their homes for any reason on the 17th day of the month.

While Muskan celebrated and was happy, the Earth Mother was angry at her for killing an innocent soul; the Earth Mother was angry at the whole village because of what Neel and Prita did, so she cursed the water town.

It turned to blood, and the whole town didn't see clean water for washing and cooking. They only had water they stored in reservoirs to use, and if that finished without the Well going back to normal, then many people would starve, and a lot more people would leave the town for other places.

The town Raja tried to find out what was wrong with the water; he sent people over to the Well to see what happened. Experts came to check the Well, but they didn't see anything wrong with it; they couldn't find a reason why the Well would be bloody.

ᑭᑭᑭ

Muskan saw Earth Mother in a dream and was told to tell the truth to everyone else or else she'd commit atrocities on them. Muskan woke up and dismissed the dream; she didn't take it seriously and ignored the Earth Mother; the Earth Mother, seeing that Muskan did this, held back the rain that was supposed to provide water for the town.

The rain didn't fall, and the plants on the farms began to die; the ground was too dry for them to survive on it. The sun also became scorching hot, beating down on the people of town every day. The people came together to make sacrifices to the Earth Mother but as soon as they approached the Well with their sacrifices, lighting struck the sky, and everyone ran way in different directions.

People went into their homes knowing the Earth Mother was angry at them, they didn't leave their homes anymore, and the school was closed down.

Muskan saw it all happen, and she still didn't think she was the cause of everything that happened in the town; the Earth Mother appeared to Muskan again, so the town could be set free.

This time Muskan took her seriously, but she was too scared to tell anyone what she did; the Earth Mother kept appearing to Muskan in her dreams, giving her nightmares until Muskan was too scared to close her eyes to sleep.

Then she started to protect hallucinations in Muskan's mind; Muskan started to see Neel and Prita wherever she went. She would scream and point, but other people couldn't see them, just her. The hallucinations got very bad that Muskan couldn't leave her room anymore; she would cry and scratch her body, trying to get rid of the hallucinating, but they didn't stop; they just kept coming harder until Muskan couldn't take it anymore. She decided to confess what she had done.

First, she called her parents and told them about her advising Neel to take Prita to the hills on the 17th. Her parents were shocked by what she did that they took her to the Raja's house immediately, where she confessed everything.

After confessing everything, the Earth Mother appeared in front of her and told her how proud she was that Muskan confessed everything.

The people saw Muskan talk to someone, but they didn't see who the person was; the Earth Mother stretched her hand to Muskan, and Muskan took it. The earth mother said she would take Muskan to a safe pace and told her to follow her.

The whole town saw Muskan walking in the town held by an invisible hand. Her parents tried to call her back, but Muskan didn't listen; she kept following the Earth Mother as she directed her; the Earth Mother took her to the Well and smiled at Muskan. She told Muskan that Neel was waiting for her at the other side, and she should go in the Well.

Seeing that Muskan would commit suicide, her mother screamed and wanted to get her, but the town Raja held her back, saying the Earth Mother was punishing her. Muskan mother has to watch in horror as Muskan climbed the Well and smiled at her, Muskan plunged into the Well, and she immediately fell to her death.

The town rushed to the Well to see Muskan's body, but it wasn't there anymore, and the well water was now clear.

Muskan mother almost ran mad when she saw what happened; her body couldn't contain the grief, so she fell and collapsed right there on the ground; she was carried home by some people and her husband. Still, the disgrace and the pain were too much for her that she and her husband moved out of the town, leaving behind their families.

The town mourned their dead, and they paid their respects to Neel's parents, who were still in the town and hadn't left yet, days went by, but the pain didn't; Neel's mother missed him every day of her life. He was her only son, although he had a sister. Neel's father couldn't bear the sight of Neel's mother anymore, so he left her and remarried another woman, while Neel's mother had to survive alone with her remaining child.

As people went, so did people who came into the town. After months of everything being normal in the town, a new family moved into Muskan's old house; they were a very large family; there were two parents and six children, one of the children was a blind boy.

The town welcomed the new family, and they were brought up to date on the town's affairs. The family used to live in the city, but they had fallen on hard times after the father lost his job, so they had to find another area to live. A friend informed them of the town, so he decided to move there to start a new life with his family.

Although they didn't have much, the townspeople tried to help them in any way they could, they gave them food as they moved in, and some of the market women found a stall for this wife so she could be trading in the marketplace.

All the six children of that family were mischievous; they were spoilt town kids who didn't want any part of this town life.

They would terrorize the neighbors by making loud rackets and stealing their chickens; they would also open the goats' house of the neighbors and let the goats out in the streets. The man next door would come home and meet his goats gone; he would scream and storm next door to comfort the family.

The children would act all innocent and hurt when he blamed it on them, and their parents would beg the man and apologize for wherever pain they might have caused him; they knew their kids was a terror, but they thought that town life might put some sense into them, and they might see the wrong of their ways, but it just made them worse.

They would throw stones at the people in the streets, push older people in the streets, and cut the rope line for clothes so the newly washed clothes would fall to the ground and be dirty. The neighbors grew tired of these children; they had never seen their kind before, especially the blind kid.

He was the troublesome one out of all of them, he was the master planner while the rest of the kids followed him, but when his plan backfires, he will act like the innocent one in the group while his siblings would get punished for his crimes. The townspeople hadn't told the children about the tradition of staying inside the houses when it was the seventeen-day of the month.

When their parents had told them about it, they began to ask questions about it.

"What is it about?" The first child asked their parents when they told them about the day.

"It is a day that the Earth Mother set aside so the well can be cleansed," their mother explained to them.

"So why do we have to stay inside?" the second child asked.

"Well because a woman is going to come from the mountains and she is going to help us purify the well," the mother explained again.

"This is a very odd tradition," the blind boy said.

"We know it is, but this is our new whole and we have to respect the traditions that have been set in place before we came here," the father said.

"So, this is why we are begging you to please listen to us and stay inside," the mother pleaded with them.

"Why?" the fourth child said, she was the only girl amongst them.

"Because if you do not stay at home, the Earth Mother is going to kill you."

"Kill us?" the children chorused.

"Yes, she killed a boy and a girl a couple of months before we arrived here. They went out on that day, and they were killed."

"Wow, that is very bad," the fifth child said.

"Yes, we know and that is why we are telling you to please stay inside. Don't try to play any pranks that day just stay put and stay inside."

"Mother, you should know us that we are calm children, it hurts our feelings that you do not trust us enough," the first child said.

"I am sorry, but we just have to make sure you do as we say," the mother said.

"Sure, we will," the first child said and stood from where he sat.

They were in the children's room; the children slept together in a room with beds on the floor.

"No need to worry, you can all go now," The first child said to his parents.

The Father and Mother left the room and hoped their children would listen to them.

"So now that they are gone, do you have a plan?" The first said.

They all turned to the blind boy who sat on his bed with a smile on his face "oh yes I do."

The children all huddled around his bed.

"Here is how it is going to; while we are all inside, we are going to make sure we leave at a time when our parents are both asleep, so I suggest we leave at night. We will lock the doors of their room, and we will sneak out of the house.

We will see what the big deal is about this Well, and then we get back inside the house," the blind boy explained.

"But what about the Earth mother, won't she kill us?" the last child asked.

"Don't tell me you believed that dear brother," the blind kid said "that was just a story to get us scared, nothing is going to happen to us if we leave. So don't worry, you can all go back to sleep now?" the blind boy said and dismissed the rest of his siblings.

They all left his bed alone and went to their beds, the 17th was tomorrow, and a plan was in the process of being executed. Only the blind son was awake after everyone else had gone to bed; he added the final touches to his plan.

ꝥꝥꝥ

The next day the children ensured they were on good behavior; they did chores for their parents and cleaned the house. By the time the woman from the mountain came to the town, they were glued to their windows and watched her.

They watched her disappear into the Well area and saw her come back outside looking very beautiful; the kids were awed. It was a brand-new experience at that time. The parents also noticed the children's behaviors and commended them later as they ate their dinners.

"You children were well behaved today, we are proud of you," the father started to say.

"Yes, we really are proud of you. We know we haven't been the best parents these days, but we know you are trying your best to adjust to this new way of life," the mother said.

"Mother we understand it is okay, we know you are trying your best to make us fit in this new town," the first child said.

"Thank you," the mother said.

They ate the rest of their dinners amidst laughter, and the children offered to do the dishes; normally, the mother does the dishes while the children go to sleep, but today the children told their parents to go to sleep when they washed the dishes.

"Are you sure you can handle it?" The mother asked them, "you are not used to doing the dishes."

"I think we can handle a couple of plates," the first child said.

The children practically pushed their parents into their room and went to take care of the dishes; after they were done with the dishes, they converged in their room for the blind boy to give them instructions.

"Okay you and you," the blind boy pointed at the fourth and fifth children" You are going to lock their room."

"You," he pointed at the second child, you are going to open the door and wait for us to come.

"You," he pointed at the last child, you are going to stay in the house and try to stall our parents in case they wake up.

"Aw, so I do not get to go on the adventure with you," the last child cried.

"It might be dangerous okay. Everyone get to your station; we are about to have an adventure."

The children went ahead to exclude their part of the plan while the first child and the blind boy waited for them to finish so they could go out.

The fourth and fifth children came for the "come on, we have locked the door." The first child left the blind boy to the front door, where the second child was waiting for them to come.

The second child locked the door behind him, leaving the last child in the house; the five of them sneaked past their house in the cover of the night they passed the backyards of the house so no one would see them.

They ran to the Well; they stood at a distance and looked at the Well.

"It doesn't look that scary," the second child said.

"How did it look? Tell me, "The blind boy said.

"It is just your typical Well, blocks plastered over each other in a round structure," the first child said.

"Is that all?" the blond boy asked.

"Yes"

"That is very disappointing," the blind boy said.

"Yes, it is let's have a closer look."

"I do not want to go there anymore. I am scared of the Well," the second child said.

"Oh, come on, don't be scared."

"I am not going there," the fourth child also said, and they stood back.

"Come on let's go," the first child said, and the rest of the kids followed him.

The first child-led the blind boy to the Well; they looked into the water and tried to see what was so special about it.

As they looked upon the water, a bright light flashed out of the water.

"Ow it hurts my eyes," the fifth child cried and crouched to the ground.

"What is going on?" the blind child asked.

"It hurts," the first child said and shouted, "we have to go home," the first child said and dragged the blind child.

The second and fourth children seeing the light, ran all the way home. The first child held the blind boy's hands all the way home, and they met the last child at the door.

"What happened?" he asked them.

"Nothing," the first child said, and they all entered the house.

The fifth child locked the door behind them, and they all went into their room silently.

"Can someone tell me what happened?" The blind boy asked.

"Don't worry about it, why did you leave us alone there?" the first child said to the second and fourth child.

"We didn't want to get into any trouble," the second child said.

"Can we all go to bed please; no one must know what's happened," the fifth child said.

They all agreed and went to bed with the first child helping the blind boy in his bed. They all went to sleep, but the blind boy laid awake rubbing at his eyes; for a slight moment, he thought he could see his hands, but he blinked, and his world went dark again.

The next morning the children all awoke and went to do their house chores before their parents awoke and noticed anything was wrong.

They all hurriedly quickly arranged the house, including making their parents breakfast, and waited for them to eat.

The blind boy was still sleeping, as they normally did in their home. The rest of the kids would wake up, and they would get the housework done while he slept, and when they were speaking, one of them would come to wake him so he could have some breakfast.

Today when they sat down for breakfast, their parents asked for the blind boy, and the first child volunteered to get him. He met the blind boy on his bed when he got to the room, staring at the wall.

"Come, everyone is waiting for you to eat breakfast," the first child said.

"Oh," the blind boy said, 'which one of them are you?" The blind boy asked.

"What do you mean which of them am I? I'm your brother."

"I know," the blind boy said. "I just want to know which one you are since I can now see you," the blind boy said, smiling.

"Wait," the first child said, shocked, "you can see me" he pointed at himself.

"Yes, I can see you," the blind boy smiled again. "You are tall, and you have dark skin, you are wearing brown shorts, and you are not wearing any shirts the blind boy described him.

"Oh, this is amazing the first child exclaimed.

"I know this is wonderful. Ever since we came back from the well, I have been feeling something in my eye and now I can see," the blind boy said.

"Oh no," the first child whispered.

"Why, what is wrong?" The blind boy asked him, seeing the look on his brother's face.

"We weren't supposed to be at the well. We were disobedient. Our parents are going to be very fruits with us."

"Nut I can see, that is a good thing," the blind said, getting on his feet. "Let's go tell the rest of the family the good news," he said cheerfully.

"Wait"

"Why?"

"Let me go tell our siblings first then we can all find a way to tell our parents what happened?" the first child said, "just want for me," the first child said.

He left the blind boy in the room and went to tell his remaining siblings what had happened.

"Uhmm, you need to come. I want to discuss something with you," the first child announced as he entered the eating area where the rest of the family was.

"What is going on?" Their father asked.

"This is siblings' business, so I will need the rest of you in your room right this instant the first child said.

"Hope nothing is wrong?" Their mother said, worried.

"No worries mama. It is all good," the first child said.

The remaining children grumbled, but they all got to their feet and followed the first child to the room.

"Behold," the first child announced as he left for the room.

The rest of the children came in after him and saw the blind boy standing with a smile on his face.

"What is going on, we have seen our brother before," the last child scoffed.

"Yes, you have but has he ever seen you before," the first child said, grinning.

The children looked at the blind boy, he was still smiling at them, and it began to dawn on them.

"You can see us?" The last child asked him quietly.

"Yes, I can," the blind boy said, laughing.

"Quick how do I look?" the last child asked him again.

"Hmm, you are short and scrawny, and you are missing a tooth," the blind boy said. "Hey, that's me," the last child said and ran to hug him.

The rest hugged him too; it was a miracle, their brother had been born blind, and now he could truly see them.

"How does it feel?" The second child asked him.

"It feels a little strange. I am still trying to get used to the sun and how bright it is," the blond boy said.

"Well, this is wonderful news, we have to tell papa and mama immediately," the second child said and walked towards the room door.

"No, we cannot do that," the first child said, stopping him.

"Why not?"

"Because our brother here was healed by the well," the first child explained.

"Oh no, that is bad," the second child gasped. "I knew we shouldn't have gone near the well, now see what had happened."

"It has happened we can't turn back in time."

"What really happened at the well" the last child asked.

"Trust me the lesser you know the better," the fifth child said, rubbing his hair.

"So, what now?" the fourth child asked.

"We have to tell our parents the truth this morning."

"How do you suggest we do that?" the second child asked.

"We are going to tell them together."

"Together, that we disobeyed them. We are going to get a serious beating this morning," the fifth child groaned.

"So what do you suggest we do? We have to tell them the truth. Mama has been trying to find a way to get our brother to see since birth but now he can see they deserve to know that. Even if we did disobey them at least for once something good came out of it."

"You are right though," the second child said. "So who is going to tell them the news because it can't be me."

"I think we all know who is going to tell them the truth," the blind boy said, smiling at the first child.

The rest of the children looked at him too.

"Oh really?" The first child asked them all.

"Well, you are the first child second child said, "do the honors," he pointed at the door.

"Fine," the first child said, storming out of the room.

He walked back to meet their parents, who were still seated, waiting for them to eat breakfast.

"What is it?" Their mother asked; seeing the first child, she rose to her feet to meet him.

"Mama, papa. We have done something really wrong and I think you need to be seated for this," he said.

"What is going on?" Their father asked him.

"Mama please sit down before I start to talk."

Their mother went back to her chair and sat down; her heart was racing as she waited for the child to speak.

"It concerns our blind Brother," the first child said.

"What happened to him, did he hit his head, and did he spill and fall. Tell me what is going on," their mother shouted.

"Calm down," their father said to her.

"No, he isn't hurt but first I have to say sorry to the two of you on behalf of me and my siblings."

"What is going on? Please tell me," Their mother asked hysterically.

"Okay so remember how you told us to stay inside yesterday because of the well thing?" The first child asked.

"Yes, we do, as a matter of fact, we have to be don where quickly becomes we are going to go over to the Raja's House for the celebration. And I trust you children stayed in like we told you to," the father said.

"Yes, we did stay in until it was night," the first child explained.

"Don't tell me, you children left the house last night. Is that why you hurriedly asked us to go to bed?"

"Yes, that is the reason why. We did leave the house last night. But we just wanted to see the well and what the big deal was."

"We told you not to leave the house, we were very clear about what was going to happen to you," the father shouting standing from where he was seated.

"Papa, I am sorry, we just wanted to see for ourselves," the first child cried.

"Look at me," the mother said, "is your brother now dead. Did the Earth Mother kill my son?" She asked him, tears running down her face.

"No, he is not dead; in fact, he is alive and well."

"Okay, so where is he?" Their mother asked.

"Here I am mama."

Their mother turned and saw the blind boy in the doorway; he was the only one standing there.

"What are you doing here? How did you get here, why is no one going you" their mother asked as she rushed to hug him?

"Mama, I don't think that will be necessary," the first child said behind her.

The rest of the children emerged behind the blind boy, smiling at her.

"What is going on?" the mother asked them.

"Mama, I can see you now," the blind boy said, smiling at her.

"You can what?" She looked at him, shocked.

"Yes mama, I can," the blind boy said.

The mother was scared as she hugged him; the father also came and looked at him; he asked him to say how many fingers he was holding up, the boy said it correctly, and his father lifted him off the floor.

Their father hugged him and cried asked did their mother, who wanted nothing more than for her son to see her with his eyes.

"How, did this happen," their mother said amidst tears.

"That is the problem. When we were at the well, a bright light came out of the well when we looked at the well. We tan immediately we saw it but apparently, it healed our brother," the first child explained.

Their father sighed, and he looked at his children.

"You have all done something in your life that has caused us a lot of trouble but this one that you have done is the biggest one ever."

"We know father and we are really sorry," the blind boy apologized.

"Normally we would give you a beating, but we can't beat you for this. You disobeyed us and did something we advised against, but you have given us a great gift. You have brought joy to us today," the father finished saying.

"So, you mean you are not angry at us?" the blind boy asked wide-eyed.

"Yes, we are not mad at you. But we are going to find a way to tell the rest of the village," the father said.

"But Father, the first child said, "We are going to be outcasts. Why can't we keep the secret to ourselves? The town doesn't have to know".

"Yes, we can keep it to ourselves, but it would be wrong to do that, and besides, we don't know if your actions could harm the town.

We have to go together as a family and tell the Raja," The mother said.

"Children, let's eat and then we get dressed. After that we are going to go over to the Raja's house and celebrate with them after the celebrations, we can then talk to the Raja and the town about what has happened," the father said.

"What is going to happen to us now mama," the blind boy asked.

"I do not know yet, but we are going to figure it out as a family," their mother said to them.

"Will the Earth Mother punish him?" The last child asked.

"I do not know," the father said, looking at his wife. He was very worried.

They ate their dinners in silence and afterward locked their home and went to the Raja's House to partake in the celebrations.

The family heard whispers of how a loud cry was heard around the well yesterday. The townspeople thought it was the evil in their Wellbeing vanquished. No one else knew what happened except the children and their parents.

Their parents steeled themselves for the confrontation that would happen. They didn't know what they would do if the townspeople decided to throw them out. They had no other place to go.

They all joined the festivities and ate and drank with the rest of the family. They tried to act like nothing was among, and they also kept the blind boy out of sight before the town could see that he could see. It took them a while to get to the Raja as he was busy greeting people and discussing them.

When it was their turn to meet them, the father took him aside and told him his family was seeking an audience with him. The Raja told them to go into his house that his wife would open the door for them and inside for him.

They went into his house and waited patiently for him to get home to them.

The Raja came in minutes later apologizing for keeping them waiting, and the fathers told them it was nothing and they were glad to wait.

"So, what is the reason you wait to speak with me?" The Raja asked the fight.

"Well as you know me and my family are still new to this town and haven't been accustomed to the tradition of your people yet," the father started to explain to him.

"Yes, I know," the Raja said, nodding his head.

"So, it won't come as a surprise that our children were asking about the Earth Mother and wanted to get to know the tradition of this town very well," the mother also chipped in.

"I know children can be very curious," the Raja said.

So now, Raja, our children have something to tell you," Their father said.

He looked at the first child and permitted him to talk to the Raja.

"Sir, we went outside our house yesterday and we went to the well," the first child said, scared.

"Go on," Raja said.

"So, as we got there, my blind brother was also there with us. We look at the well and a bright light came out, we ran immediately we saw the light and we all ran home. Now we woke up and found that my blind brother can now see," the first child explained.

"Is that true?" The Raja asked the blind boy who was seated beside their parents.

"Yes, it is true," the blind boy said.

The Raja sighed and looked at the family.

"Never in their town has the ever happened," he stated to say.

"Yes, we know and we will also understand if you want to throw us out of the town," the mother said "our children disobeyed us but they gave us something far greater. You might tell us to eave, and we will pack out things and depart."

"Leave, I cannot ask you to leave." The Raja said.

"What why," the mother asked him.

"You have no other place to go, and there are some things that you don't know about," the Raja said "they will be revealed to you and the town today when the festivities are over.

Please do kindly join us outside," Raja said and attached his hand to the blind boy "come on, let's go and meet the people."

The Raja led the blind boy outside of the house, and when the people saw that the boy could see, they gasped and went forward to him and asked what happened.

"Today, a miracle has happened in our village and it is the courtesy of one family," the Raja said.

The rest of the family stepped up behind the Raja and looked at the townspeople.

"Go ahead son" the Raja nudged the first child.

"Say what happened."

The boy timidly looked upon everybody and talked about what had happened for the third time that day. After he finished, the townspeople looked at the family with disgust.

They started to clamor to leave the town, but the Raja told them. Would you please calm down and listen to him?

"The Earth mother appeared to me in a dream and told me all about this. I knew this was going to happen. I just had to wait for it to unfold." the Raja said.

"Why are the children not dead yet?" The townspeople asked.

"That is the mystery that won't be explained by me but by her," Raja said and pointed into the distance.

Although the townspeople couldn't see what was coming, they knew who it was already. The woman came into the town to help them; with her were the two men who had gone in search of her tribe and got captured. She had returned them home.

The woman walked into the town, and the townspeople formed a circle around her. They watched her as she spoke; they didn't understand her language, so one of the men translated for her. She spoke this.

"Hear me for I speak for this Earth Mother. I came here to tell you that a great evil happened recently on this land. A girl made Muskan deny her friend Neel and Prita. She laid in wait for them and slaughtered the two of them and returned to her house. Pretending she didn't know a thing about what happened. I was furious and got her to confess then I made her throw herself down the well because she didn't deserve to be kings the living. As for the blind boy, the water could cure sickness if the sick looked upon it on the seventeenth day of the month. So, cure your sick ones on this day" the woman stopped talking.

She looked around at the townspeople who suspected she was done talking; she started to walk back in the direction she had come in, and the two men followed her. The Raja told them to continue the festivities because they were celebrating two things: finding the truth and the blind boy who could now see.

They continued tonight, and the mother of the blond boy didn't allow him out of her sight in fear that the Earth

Mother might take his sight away from him again. So there you go; this is a very beautiful take, how years of history came together to favor one family.

Goodbye, till we meet again.

9 798885 218740

Printed by Libri Plureos GmbH in Hamburg,
Germany